READY?

PRESS HERE AND TURN THE PAGE.

GREAT! NOW PRESS THE YELLOW DOT AGAIN.

PERFECT. RUB THE DOT ON THE LEFT...
GENTLY.

WELL DONE! AND NOW THE ONE ON THE RIGHT...
GENTLY.

FABULOUS! FIVE QUICK TAPS ON THE YELLOW...

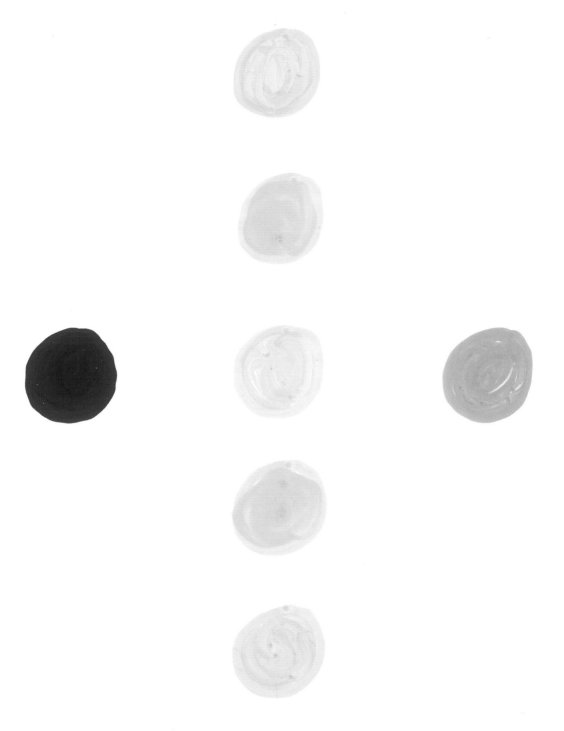

AND FIVE TAPS ON THE RED...

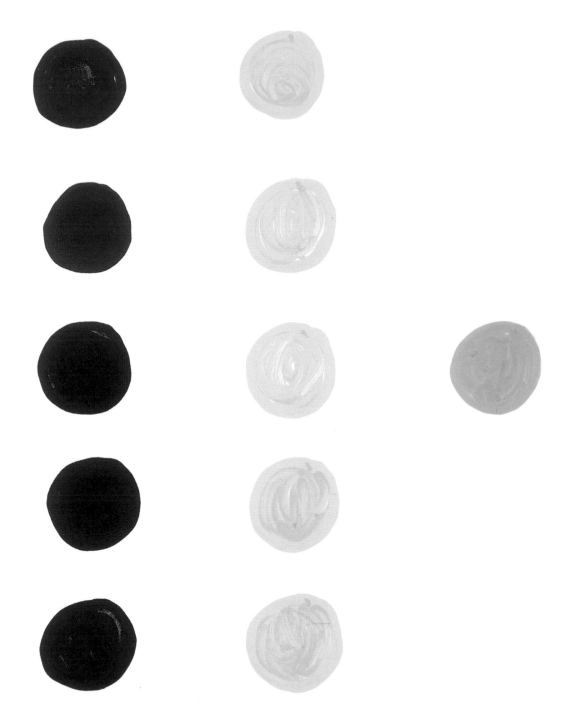

AND FINALLY FIVE TAPS ON THE BLUE.

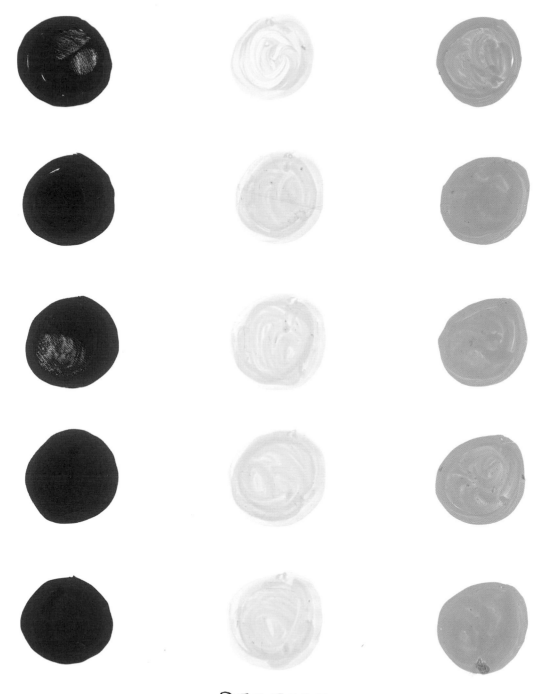

PERFECT.
TRY SHAKING THE BOOK ... JUST A LITTLE BIT.

NOT BAD. BUT MAYBE A LITTLE BIT HARDER.

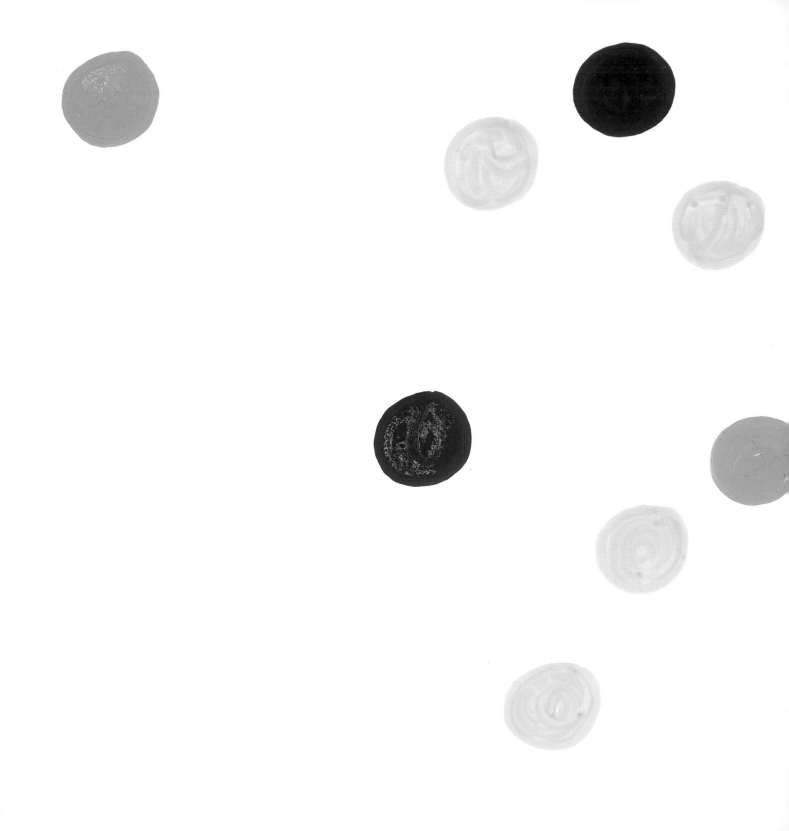

THERE. WELL DONE.
NOW TILT THE PAGE TO THE LEFT...
JUST TO SEE WHAT HAPPENS.

AND THEN TO THE RIGHT... A LITTLE MORE.

EXCELLENT!
SHAKE THE BOOK ONE MORE TIME
JUST TO GET EVERYTHING BACK IN ORDER.

HMMMM. INTERESTING.
TRY PRESSING DOWN REALLY HARD
ON **ALL** THE YELLOW DOTS.

THAT'S FUNNY!
TURN THE LIGHTS BACK ON.
TRY PRESSING THEM ALL AGAIN.

PERFECT!

(HOLD ON. TWO OF THOSE DOTS SEEM TO HAVE SWITCHED PLACES. BUT WHICH ONES?)

NOW PRESS HARD ON ALL THE DOTS. REALLY HARD.

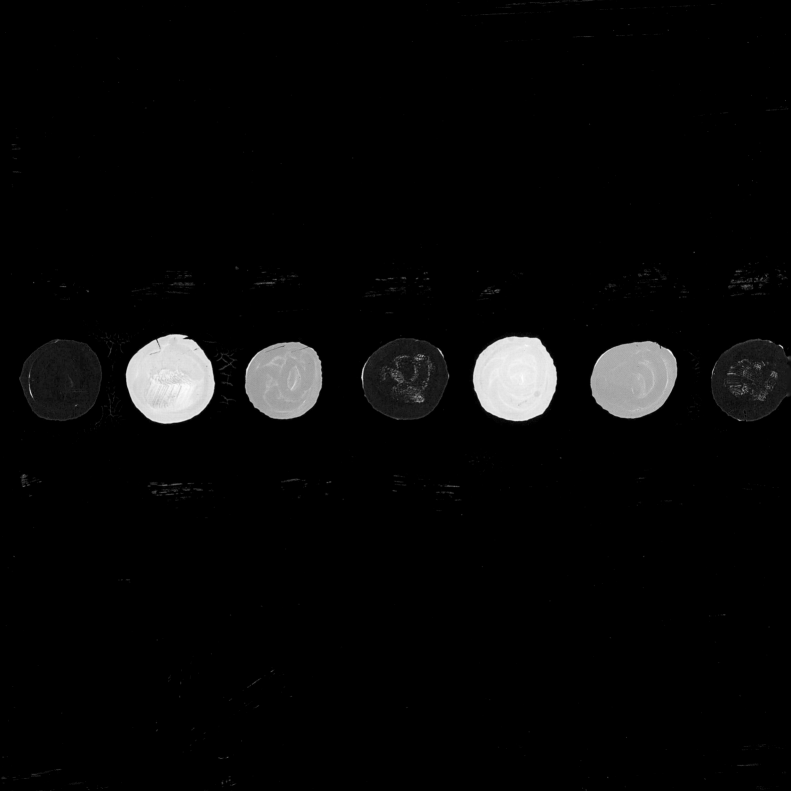

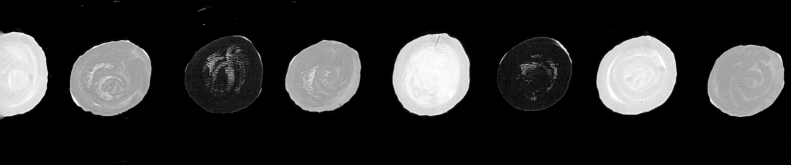

NOT BAD. SHAKE THEM UP A LITTLE.

PRETTY, ISN'T IT? TRY BLOWING ON THEM...
TO GET RID OF THE BLACK.

HMMMM. MAYBE A BIT HARDER?

Oooops. That might have been
a little bit too hard.

Stand the book up straight
to make those dots drop down again.

THERE YOU GO!
THAT'S PERFECT! NOW, CLAP YOUR HANDS ONCE.

WHOA! CLAP TWICE?

THREE TIMES?

MORE!

WHOO-HOO! KEEP CLAPPING!

MORE, MORE!

UH-OH, TOO LOUD!
QUICK, PRESS THE WHITE DOT.

BACK TO THE BEGINNING. THIS WAY . . . . ←

BRAVO!
WANT TO DO IT ALL OVER AGAIN?

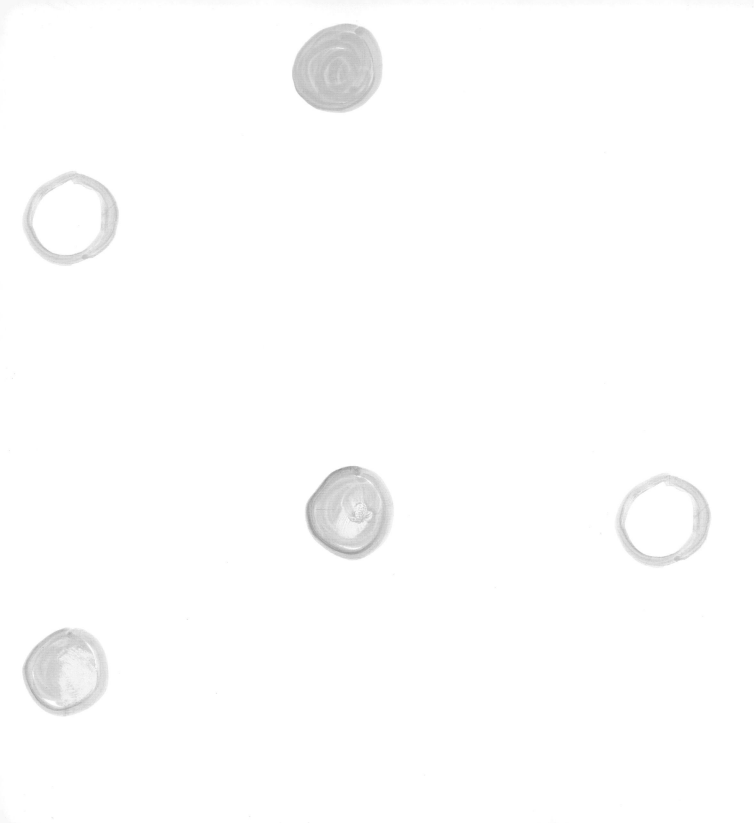

FIRST PUBLISHED IN THE UNITED STATES IN 2011
BY CHRONICLE BOOKS LLC.

COPYRIGHT © 2010 BY BAYARD EDITIONS.
ORIGINALLY PUBLISHED IN FRANCE IN 2010
BY BAYARD EDITIONS UNDER THE TITLE "UN LIVRE."

TRANSLATED BY CHRISTOPHER FRANCESCHELLI.

LIBRARY OF CONGRESS CATALOGING-IN-PUBLICATION DATA AVAILABLE.
ISBN 978-0-8118-7954-5

MANUFACTURED BY TOPPAN LEEFUNG,
DONGGUAN, CHINA, IN SEPTEMBER 2012

10 9 8 7

THIS PRODUCT CONFORMS TO CPSIA 2008.

HANDPRINT BOOKS
AN IMPRINT OF CHRONICLE BOOKS
680 SECOND STREET
SAN FRANCISCO, CA 94107
WWW.CHRONICLEKIDS.COM

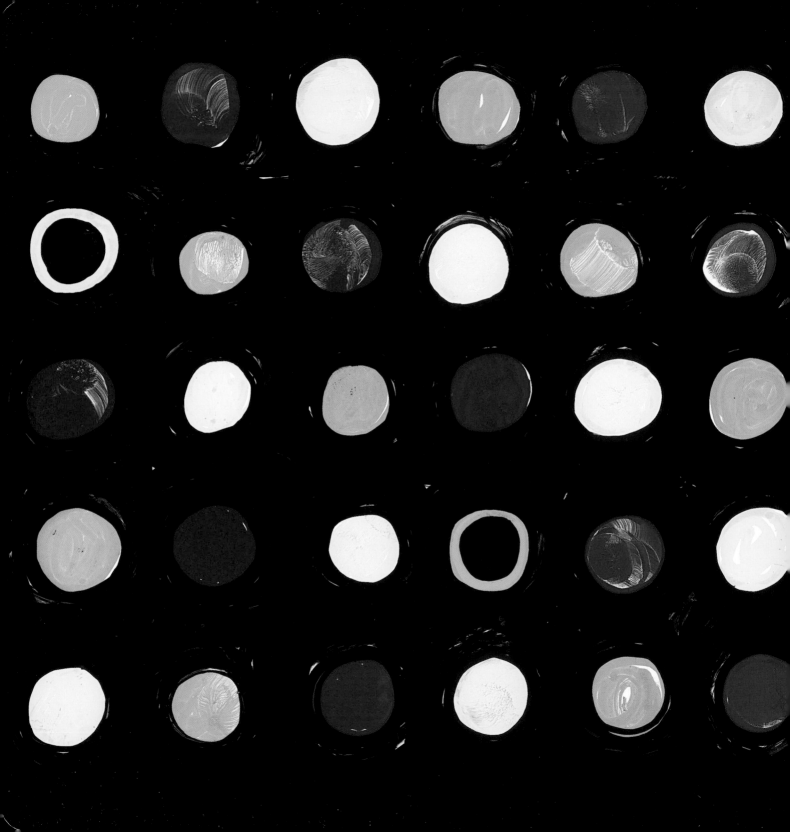